a clutter,

a mess.

Milly, Molly and Heidi Untidy

"We may look different
but we feel the same."

Milly and Molly's friend Heidi Untidy lived
in a jumble,

It grew.

It got bigger.

It took on a life of its own.

"Tidy it up", said her mother
"But where do I start?" asked Heidi.

"Just start," said her mother and closed the
door tight, to stop it from all getting out.

Heidi Untidy didn't know where to start, so
she curled up in it all and she read.

Now Heidi Untidy was a reader. She read
to her mother.

She read to her father.

She read to her brother and sister

and anyone who cared to listen.

She liked some books better than others
and she liked one book best of all.

"Where's my best book?" she cried.

"It's buried. It's smothered. You've drowned it,"
said her mother.

"Tidy it up", said her mother
"But where do I start?" asked Heidi.

"Just start," said her mother and closed the door tight, to stop it from all getting out.

So Heidi Untidy made a start.

She folded and stacked and stacked and tidied
and folded and stacked some more.

"I've found it alive. My best book," she cried.

"Heidi, you're tidy!" said her mother.

Milly and Molly's friend Heidi Untidy was
never untidy again.